Salty Sea Stories!

Imagination Day

It's another bright, sunny morning in Bikini Bottom. SpongeBob SquarePants and his best friend Patrick Star are **eagerly awaiting** a special **delivery** from the mail truck.

Finally! The mailman delivers a huge package **addressed** to Mr. SquarePants! SpongeBob and Patrick **carefully** open the box, take out an **enormous** TV, and **toss** it in the trash! Then they jump into the empty box.

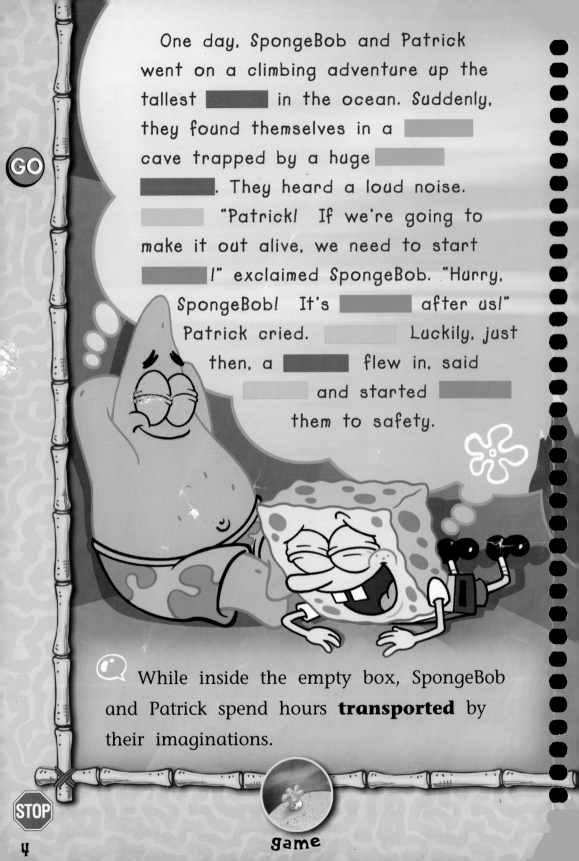

One day, SpongeBob and Patrick went on a climbing adventure up the tallest ▮▮▮▮▮ in the ocean. Suddenly, they found themselves in a ▮▮▮▮▮ cave trapped by a huge ▮▮▮▮▮ ▮▮▮▮▮. They heard a loud noise. ▮▮▮▮▮ "Patrick! If we're going to make it out alive, we need to start ▮▮▮▮▮!" exclaimed SpongeBob. "Hurry, SpongeBob! It's ▮▮▮▮▮ after us!" Patrick cried. ▮▮▮▮▮ Luckily, just then, a ▮▮▮▮▮ flew in, said ▮▮▮▮▮ and started ▮▮▮▮▮ them to safety.

While inside the empty box, SpongeBob and Patrick spend hours **transported** by their imaginations.

GO

STOP

game

4

Nouns
sneaker
tiger
clam
wizard
television
bunny
donut

Sound Effects

Adjectives
dark
scary
gross
stinky
hairy
cute
fluffy

Verbs
eating
dancing
running
singing
laughing
jumping
flying

Squidward is **annoyed.** SpongeBob and Patrick are having too much fun in their **cardboard** box.

GO

STOP

games   level 1   level 2

6

How can SpongeBob and Patrick make so much noise with just an empty box? Squidward hops in to find out.

Squidward can't understand it. He has a **gigantic** new TV, but SpongeBob and Patrick are having more fun inside the empty box than he is watching television!

Frustrated, Squidward tries his own imagination out in an old hat box, but it doesn't work.

SpongeBob and Patrick, **exhausted** from a long and **satisfying** day of imagining, go home to rest. Squidward sees his **opportunity** and sneaks into the box. But there are no knobs, levers, or buttons. There's no tape recorder or radio. There's only one **conclusion**! Squidward finally **decides** to try it.

GARBAGE

GO

STOP

Squidward is **amazed**! He can hear the engine **revving**, he can feel the car **accelerating**, and he can smell the...

...GARBAGE? Squidward's been dumped!

THE END

game

repeat

Wormy!

Sandy Cheeks has gone out of town and left SpongeBob and Patrick **in charge** of **pet sitting** while she's away.

Dear SpongeBob and Patrick,

Howdy! Thanks for taking care of my critters!

Every day, please give Birdie some seed, Snakey one gerbil, and Cricket a few ants.

Have fun!

Your friend,
Sandy Cheeks

PS: That little guy in the jar is Wormy. Don't worry about him - he doesn't eat much.

BIRDSEED

SpongeBob and Patrick play all day with their new best friend, Wormy. Hide and Seek is the most **popular** game, but sometimes Wormy is *too* good at hiding!

sea

mail

sail

cup

fish

chalk

jelly

boat

-er

-ed

-ing

un-

re-

do

cover

cake

light

board

shore

man

shell

net

dark

horse

box

GO

STOP

games

level 1

level 2

At the end of the day, it **breaks their hearts** to say goodbye.

That night, something very **exciting** happens. Wormy **metamorphoses** into a butterfly!

The next day, SpongeBob and Patrick **return** to the Treedome. But their new best friend is gone...

GO

and **instead** they find a **horrifying** MONSTER!

STOP

16

The Monster must have eaten Wormy! SpongeBob and Patrick are afraid that it will eat them, or Sandy's other pets, next! They have to find a way to **protect** the **innocent creatures** in the Treedome.

3/8	36	4	9	56
5	25	14	1/2	63
0	8	49	1	11

SpongeBob and Patrick are **successful**, and the Monster flies out of the Treedome. But now it is headed toward Bikini Bottom!

GO

STOP

game

18

When the **citizens** hear the **urgent warning**, they are **terrified**. **Chaos** breaks out!

In the **nick of time**, Sandy Cheeks returns from her vacation and catches the Monster. Then she **reveals** that the Monster is **actually** their new best friend Wormy!

JellyFish

GO

STOP

22

game 1   game 2

Discoveries at every age!

Four levels of interactive *LeapPad®* books enhance skills in reading, math and other essential subjects, with colorful stories and activities. Utilizing our patented NearTouch® technology, each page comes alive with engaging and instructional interactivity that makes learning fun!

Pre-Reading, Pre-Math and Essential Subjects
Picture Books and Activity Books

LeapStart books introduce your child to the building blocks of math, reading, and other subjects to successfully prepare your child for school. LeapStart books bring lessons to life with stories, music and fun activities.

Phonics Lessons and Activities
Storybooks and Activity Books

LeapPad Phonics Program is an integrated, step-by-step approach to teaching your child phonics – the key for learning to read. The lesson books help your child learn the concepts, while the activity books provide important practice to learn to read.

Reading, Math and Essential Subjects
Storybooks and Activity Books

Leap 1 helps your child build a foundation in reading, math and other essential subjects. Leap 1 books also help increase your child's vocabulary with engaging stories and activities.

Reading Comprehension and Reading to Learn
First Chapter Books and Subject-Based Books

Leap 2 introduces your child to chapter books that help strengthen vocabulary and reading comprehension skills. Leap 2 also expands your child's knowledge with books that help teach math, science, music and more!

Look for other great LEAP•2 interactive books!

Arthur and the Lost Diary
© 1998 Marc Brown

Hit it, Maestro!

Disney/Pixar Monsters, Inc.
© 2001 Disney/Pixar

The Great Dune Buggy Race

Scooby-Doo and the Zombie's Treasure
TM & © Hanna-Barbera
TM & © Cartoon Network (s02)

Amazing Mammals

First Chapter Books:
Arthur and the Lost Diary
Arthur Makes the Team
Scooby-Doo and the Haunted Castle
Scooby-Doo and the Zombie's Treasure

Activity Storybook:
Disney/Pixar Monsters, Inc.
Superman

Math:
The Great Dune Buggy Race

Science:
I Know Where My Food Goes
Amazing Mammals

Music:
Hit it, Maestro!

Go to www.leapfrog.com to see our complete library of LeapPad books

* U.S.Toy Retail Sales Tracking Service, 2000 and 2001
** Not all books available in Canada.